A Rainbow OF Friends

A Book to Celebrate Diversity

P. K. Hallinan

ideals children's books™
Nashville, Tennessee

ISBN 0-8249-5394-0 (case)
ISBN 0-8249-5395-9 (paper)

Published by Ideals Children's Books
An imprint of Ideals Publications
A division of Guideposts
535 Metroplex Drive, Suite 250
Nashville, Tennessee 37211
www.IdealsBooks.com

Printed and bound in Mexico by RR Donnelley & Sons.

Library of Congress Cataloging-in-Publication Data
Hallinan, P.K.
    A rainbow of friends / written and illustrated by P.K. Hallinan.
        p.   cm.
    Summary: A story in verse about how all friends are special and valuable regardless of
    differences or difficulties.
    [1. Friendship—Fiction. 2. Multiculturalism—Fiction. 3. Stories in rhyme.]
  I. Title.
  PZ8.3.H15Ra1   1994
  [E]—dc20   93-39257
                                      CIP
                                      AC

For my rainbow of friends—the children of this earth.

Books by P. K. Hallinan

A Rainbow of Friends

For the Love of Our Earth

Heartprints

How Do I Love You?

I'm Thankful Each Day!

Just Open a Book

Let's Learn All We Can!

My Dentist, My Friend

My Doctor, My Friend

My First Day of School

My Teacher's My Friend

That's What a Friend Is

Today Is Christmas!

Today Is Easter!

Today Is Halloween!

Today Is Thanksgiving!

Today Is Valentine's Day!

Today Is Your Birthday!

We're Very Good Friends, My Brother and I

We're Very Good Friends, My Father and I

We're Very Good Friends, My Grandma and I

We're Very Good Friends, My Grandpa and I

We're Very Good Friends, My Mother and I

We're Very Good Friends, My Sister and I

When I Grow Up

10 9 8 7 6 5 4 3 2 1

A rainbow of friends
is the vision we see
when we think about peace
and world harmony.

Some friends are funny.

Some friends are stars.

Some friends wear clothing
that's different from ours.

But all friends are special
and add in some way
to the richness of life—
how we think, what we say.

A rainbow of friends
is a dream we can share
where everyone's treated
with kindness and care.

A friend may be challenged
in movement or speech.

A friend may be distant
or difficult to reach.

Still, each friend is given
a share of our hearts,
so no one feels different,
unloved, or apart.

A rainbow of friends
is a chance for us all
to help one another
when we stumble or fall.

We all have our interests.

We all have our views.

We all have our strengths
and our weaknesses too.

And though we may wander
a bit wide or far,
our friends still accept us
the way that we are.

A rainbow of friends
is a bonding together
that eases our journey
through all kinds of weather.

If we work hand in hand,
all jobs can be done.

Our goals can be reached
with the greatest success
by trusting that others
are doing their best.

So reach out with love
to the people you meet,
and offer a smile
to all those you greet.

The world is a family
whose happiness depends
on a circle of caring . . .

on a rainbow of friends.